Game of Scones

By Eric Luper

Illustrated by
"The Doodle Boy" Joe Whale

Scholastic Inc.

All rights reserved. Published by Scholastic Inc., *Publishers since 1920.* SCHOLASTIC and associated logos are trademarks and/or registered trademarks of Scholastic Inc.

The publisher does not have any control over and does not assume any responsibility for author or third-party websites or their content.

This book is a work of fiction. Names, characters, places, and incidents are either the product of the author's imagination or are used fictitiously, and any resemblance to actual persons, living or dead, business establishments, events, or locales is entirely coincidental.

ISBN 978-1-338-73035-7

1 2021

Printed in the U.S.A.   23

First printing 2021

Book design by Veronica Mang

SCHOOL MAP

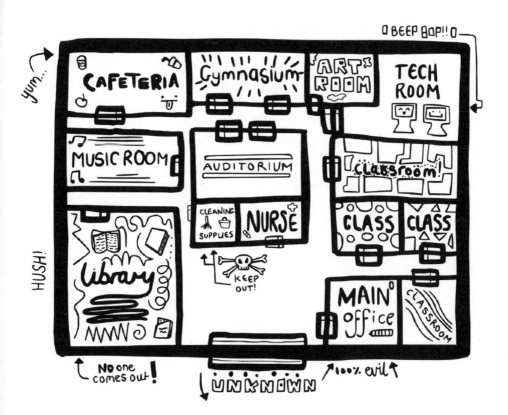

CHAPTER 1
The Way It's Always Bean

In many ways, Belching Walrus Elementary is probably similar to your school. There is a flagpole with a flappy flag in front. There are big heavy doors that slam shut when you walk in. There are hallways that lead to different classrooms. There is an auditorium with a stage, a gymnasium with sports equipment, and a library with books. There is a cafeteria where the food lives. And, just like in

your school, after all the doors are locked, the food in the cafeteria comes alive to party.

What's that, you say? The food in your cafeteria *doesn't* come alive each night to party? Well, next time you get a chance, grab your sleeping bag and a flashlight and camp out under one of the lunch tables for the evening. You'll see.

Note: When you do camp out in your school's cafeteria, be sure to bring your own food. Not only is eating the food from your cafeteria without paying for it stealing, but the food will run away before you have a chance to pop it in your mouth.

So before you read any further, you should get to know some of the folks who live at Belching Walrus Elementary. I mean, if you don't like our characters, you might not want to read on. You might want to toss this book over your shoulder and move on to something more your speed. Bench-pressing kittens? Snowshoeing through the Alps with a yeti? Skydiving with a silverback gorilla? Hey, whatever browns your toast.

Slice

Food Type: Slice of pizza

Flavor: Cheesy

Personality: Chipper and always positive

Strengths: Boundless energy, ultra-friendly

Weaknesses: Fear of the microwave (it makes him soggy) and mice (they like cheese)

Hobbies: He's not sure . . .

Scoop

Food Type: Triple scoop ice cream cone

Flavor: Vanilla, chocolate, and strawberry

Personality: Super sweet, but also super focused

Strengths: Planning and strategy

Weaknesses: Can be melty at times

Catchphrase: "That's driptastic!" (Actually, she never says that. It's silly.)

Hobbies: Painting and graffiti

Totz

Food Type: Tater tot (don't call him a "Potato Puff"—
that's what they call his granddad)

Flavor: Delicious!

Personality: Laid-back, but trendy

Strengths: Spitting mad rhymes

Weaknesses: Fear of the deep fryer, fear of public
speaking

Hobbies: Spoken-word poetry

Of course, there are plenty of other folks in the Belching Walrus Elementary Cafeteria—baskets filled with fruits, a huge jar of pickles, a Cooler filled with chocolate milks and apple juices, and a freezer filled with ice pops and yet-to-be-nuked chicken nugs—but you'll learn about them as the story

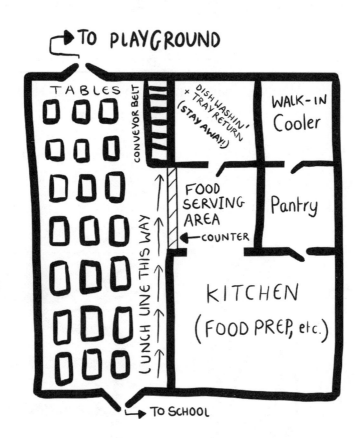

unfolds. Right now, just know that Slice, Scoop, and Totz, as usual, were hanging out under the lunchroom sink.

And not one of them knew their perfect lives were about to change forever.

CHAPTER 2

Spitting Rhymes, Changing Times

Hey, Totz," **Slice said.** "Have you written any new rhymes?"

Totz shrugged. "I'm working on some stuff."

"Give us a sample," Scoop said as she outlined the ice cream graffiti mural she was tagging on the wall with lines of vanilla ice cream.

If a tater tot could blush, Totz would have been beet red. "Nah, it's garbage."

"Come on," Scoop said. "When I do my art, it's there for everyone to see."

"What if I go first?" Slice said.

Totz laughed. "Psssh, you can't rhyme."

"Sure I can." Slice climbed onto a small box, puffed out his cheesy chest, and gave it a try:

"My name is Slice.
Umm . . . I'm afraid of mice.
I make up words.
Like . . . uhh . . . Beezle-bice!"

Totz and Scoop laughed.

"You can't invent a word just to make it rhyme," Scoop said.

"I just did," Slice replied, hopping off the box. He nudged Totz. "Your turn."

Totz did not get onto the box. He looked to make

sure no one was around, held one hand to his head-
phones, and began swaying back and forth. Then the
words poured from his mouth, sweet as honey.

"I was raised on hard tile and cold stainless steel.
Step back or my friends will balance your meal.
I'm colder than Tasty Pops, frozen yogurt, and ice.
My rhymes are hotter than six bowls of fried rice.
Richer than butter, crunchy as nuts.
Tastier than a pound of fresh cold cuts.
My words are freshest, yours are expired.
So, get out of my frying pan and into the fryer."

Slice and Scoop burst into applause.

"That was great!" Slice said. "You should be in a talent show."

Totz shook his head. "I'd look like a fool."

"You wouldn't look like a fool," Scoop said. "You'd win."

But Totz only leaned against the leg of the sink, pulled out his tiny notebook, and wrote more rhymes.

Just then, a loud knock sounded at the door of the Pantry.

THOOM, THOOM, THOOM!

Now, this may not seem out of the ordinary to you, but for food in the Cafeteria at Belching Walrus Elementary, this was highly unusual. As long as any morsel could remember, no one had ever knocked on the door of the Pantry.

The knocking sounded again, this time louder.

"SOMEONE OPEN THE DOOR!" The grizzled old voice came from Glizzy, the grizzled old hot dog who lived in a box at the back of the Cooler. Not a single slice of cheese or crunchy carrot stick knew of anyone older than Glizzy. He limped out of the shadows and pointed a grizzled old finger at the towering door. Glizzy was so old, he wasn't red anymore. He was a pale, wrinkly gray. His mustard had long since crusted, and his foil wrapper dragged behind him in tatters.

"I said . . . open . . . the door," Glizzy said.

Slice nudged Scoop. "Hey, is a hot dog a sandwich?" he whispered.

"Huh?"

"Just wondering if a hot dog counts as a sandwich. I mean, it's meat between bread."

"I don't think so," Scoop said. "A hot dog is on a bun."

"A hamburger is on a bun and that's a sandwich," Slice said.

"A hamburger is *not* a sandwich," Scoop said. "It's got its own part on a menu, separate from sandwiches. Plus, a hot dog's bun is connected."

"A submarine sandwich is a sandwich and the bread is connected," Totz said. "I think a hot dog is a sandwich."

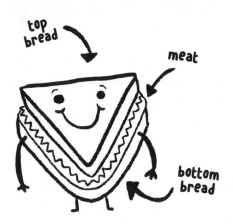

top
bread

meat

bottom
bread

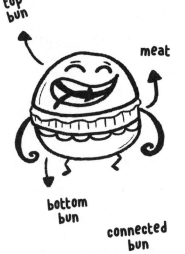

top
bun

meat

bottom
bun

connected
bun

meat

"Nope," Scoop said. "A hot dog is something different."

Finally, a dented apple waddled over to the door and pulled.

The door slowly creaked open.

In front of them stood an array of office supplies: two staplers, a paperweight, and a line of red pens. A pair of scissors crept around like a spider, its pointy tips making a clicking sound on the tile. Behind them, tallest of all, stood a yellow ruler.

"My name is Baron von Lineal," said the ruler.

"HIS NAME IS BARON VON LINEAL!" yelled a stapler.

"I am the ruler of this land."

"HE IS THE RULER OF—"

"Be quiet!" Baron von Lineal barked.

The stapler stepped back and Lineal went on. "We work harder than anyone at Belching Walrus

Elementary. Rulers measure. Staplers staple. Scissors snip. Pens write."

A large brass paperweight that looked like a fat duck waddled forward and nudged Baron von Lineal. "Oh, and paperweights . . . uh . . . sit. Anyhow, the air conditioner is broken and it is hot in the Main Office. You will let us come into the Cooler each night so we can . . . chill out."

A murmur spread across the Pantry. It spread from the pickles to the pears, from the peaches to the peanuts, from the Popsicles to the potatoes. Now, if you don't know what a murmur is, it's the sound of voices so low it sounds like this . . . "Murmur."

"Has anything like this ever happened before?" Slice whispered.

Scoop shook her head. "Not that I know of."

A pink frosted donut stepped forward next to Glizzy. She dropped sprinkles wherever she went. "This is very unusual," Sprinkles said. "We have never—"

"We don't *want* to come here," Baron von Lineal said. "It's just until the air conditioner is fixed. Your

SHARING IS CARING!

lives will not change, and there is enough room for everyone. Anyhow, your poster says it all."

Sprinkles lost a few more sprinkles.

"You'll have to give us some time to decide," Glizzy said.

"There is no time!" Lineal snapped. "We will be here tomorrow!"

The Pantry door slammed shut.

Murmurs started again.

"This doesn't feel right," Scoop said.

"Not cool," Totz mumbled.

"I like meeting new friends," Slice said. "Maybe this won't be a huge disaster."

CHAPTER 3

It Was a Huge Disaster

It was a huge disaster. The very next day, the office supplies from the Main Office showed up. Highlighter was playing music so loud, Slice could barely hear Scoop complaining. Pencils swam in the ketchup.

MANE OFFISS PARTEE ZONE

Staplers played hockey with the ice cubes. Paper clips danced around everywhere. And Magic Marker left his mark on the Cooler door.

Meanwhile, Baron von Lineal leaned against the shelves, smiling.

"This doesn't feel right," Scoop said over the music.

"Not cool," Totz mumbled.

"Come on," Slice said. He clapped his hands to the beat. "Who doesn't love parties?"

But deep down, Slice was uneasy, too. It was one thing to have a good time, but this seemed out of control.

"Maybe we should talk to Baron von Lineal," Scoop suggested.

Slice agreed. But when they tried to walk over to him, two staplers stood in the way.

"No one speaks to Baron von Lineal without an appointment," one of the staplers barked.

"Yeah, what he said," the other stapler added.

"When *can* we see him?" Totz asked.

"Tuesday," the first stapler said. "Of next year."

Both staplers laughed and turned away.

Just then, they heard something from above. Somehow, Ducky had climbed to the top shelf and was standing next to a huge jar of pickles. As he waddled to the edge, the pickles wobbled.

Ducky flapped his tiny wings and waggled his tail, but he waggled a little too much. The jar of pickles slid from the top shelf and fell.

Now, ducks may be able to fly, but pickles cannot—especially when they are trapped inside a jar. The jar fell to the tile and smashed. Broken glass and pickle juice flew everywhere. And dozens of pickles lay on the floor, flipping like fish out of water.

Okay, you may not have known that pickles can't fly, but I'm sure you knew they can't breathe regular air. They can only breathe pickle juice. So, in addition to *flipping* like fish out of water, the pickles were

CRUNCH

GHERKIN

BUMPS

FLIPPER

JUICIUS

BOB

CHILLZ

MR. BIG

PHIL

also *gasping* like fish out of water.

"We have to save them!" Slice called out, but no one knew what to do.

"Grab a bucket," he told Scoop. "And find a bottle of vinegar."

He turned to Totz. "Get some salt, and make it quick."

Slice climbed onto the sink and pulled the spray hose over the edge. He turned on the water and filled a bucket. He called out to Scoop and Totz.

"Dump in the salt and vinegar!"

As his friends added their ingredients, Slice tossed pickles into the bucket. As soon as they landed in the juice, the pickles sprang back to life, swimming around the brine like happy spaghetti.

"Thanks, Slice!" one pickle said.

"Yeah, thanks!" another called out.

Soon, all the pickles were showing their thanks.

"This must stop!" It was Glizzy, who had climbed down from his box at the back of the Cooler. "Baron von Lineal, we were kind enough to share our Cooler with you. Learn to behave, or you are not welcome here."

Baron von Lineal raised one eyebrow, which was

really the only eyebrow he had. "By my measure, you have no choice. See you tomorrow."

And with that, the office supplies marched out of the Pantry and disappeared.

Slice looked around at the destruction. Ketchup was splattered across the wall. Grapes were squished on the floor. Plastic forks were in pieces and Popsicles were melting in the corner. Sprinkle's sprinkles littered the whole Pantry.

"This is only going to get worse," Slice said. "We're going to need some help."

"To clean up?" Scoop asked.

"No, to fight Baron von Lineal. Now that he's here, he's never going to leave."

"But who is going to help us?" Totz said.

"I don't know," Slice answered. "But we have to try."

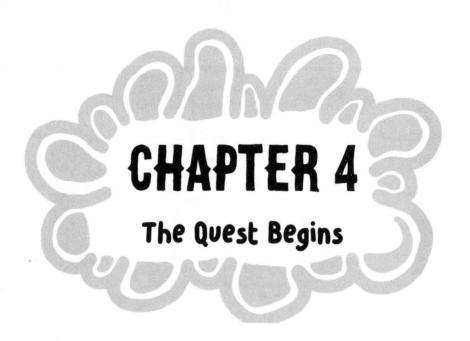

CHAPTER 4

The Quest Begins

The very next night, Slice, Scoop, and Totz slipped out of the Pantry. The Cafeteria was filled with chairs and long tables. At one end stood another doorway.

"I guess we go that way," Slice said.

As they walked, Slice started thinking about sandwiches again. "What about soft tacos?" he asked. "That's meat between bread."

"A tortilla is not bread," Scoop said.

"It seems like bread to me," Totz said.

"Soft tacos are NOT a sandwich!" Scoop insisted. "Neither are hot dogs!"

"I think they are," Totz said. "So is a slice of pizza folded in half."

"Ugh, you can be so annoying," Scoop said. She wiped a long drip of ice cream from her eyes. "Hey, is it warm out here?"

Slice and Totz ignored her and they went to the doorway.

"Guys, I'm feeling really warm," Scoop said, dripping on the floor.

"Oh gosh," Slice said. "Are you okay?"

"I'd better get back to the Cooler," she said. "I will stay near the intercom so I can talk to you. If you need anything, just press the big button and let me know."

GUYS...

Before Slice had a chance to say anything else, Scoop was gone. She left long trails of chocolate, vanilla, and strawberry streaked across the floor.

Slice and Totz continued down the hallway. The lights buzzed and flickered above them.

"Creepy," Totz said. He pulled out his notepad and started jotting down notes.

They crept down the hallway and then down another. Slice heard marching in the distance. They peered around the next corner. Hundreds of office supplies were coming down the hallway. In front, Baron von Lineal rode atop Ducky followed by a row of staplers. Behind them marched perfect rows

of pens, pencils, highlighters, and paper clips. Snip the scissors darted this way and that.

"Hide!" Slice whispered.

"There's no place to go," Totz said, looking around.

Suddenly, someone grabbed them and pulled them behind a radiator. It was Glizzy! He was wrapped in a new bun and foil and held a packet of mustard under one arm.

He held one finger over his lips to hush them as the army marched past.

"What are you doing here?" Slice asked Glizzy after the last thumbtack waddled away.

"Same as you, I reckon. I'm looking for help to fight Baron von Lineal. I haven't been this far from the Pantry since the Great School Cookout."

"The what?" Totz asked.

"The Great School Cookout." Glizzy looked into the distance and answered in a raspy voice. "It was a long time ago. Hundreds of us were brought out to a very bright place. Hot dogs, water bottles, bags of chips, ice pops. Only a few returned. They called us the Leftovers. I've been living at the back of the Cooler ever since. Don't like large crowds or bright lights no more. I keep to myself, mostly."

Slice didn't know what to say. He'd always figured Glizzy was just a mean old wrinkled hot dog.

"Follow me," Glizzy said. "We'll find help in the Art Room. Old François owes me a favor."

Glizzy led them down a hallway and through a door. The room was filled with easels and canvases. The floor was splattered with paint.

"François!" Glizzy called out. "Marquis de Pigment, Viscount of Vibrant, Duke of Color. We ask for a moment of your time!"

Magic markers squeaked, crayons buzzed, tubs of paint stirred. Finally, a single paintbrush hopped out of a cup and came forward.

"Eet has been a long time, Monsieur Glizzy," François said. "What brings you to my studio?"

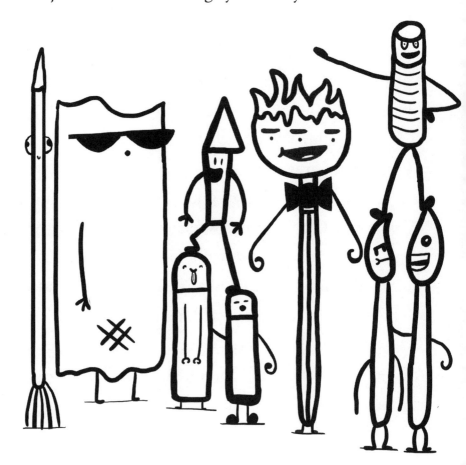

"We need your help," Glizzy explained. "Baron von Lineal has invaded our Cooler. We can't stop him ourselves."

"Zat is no concern of mine!" François said. "In fact, zis may be for ze best. Lineal has been taking paper from our closet. Perhaps he will forget about us. Now begone from my room!"

Glizzy stepped forward. "There was a time, François, when we were friends, when—"

5 days is a long time in the life span of food!

"Zose times are long ago—four or five days at least," François barked. "I said BEGONE!"

Slice, Glizzy, and Totz left.

"That paintbrush sure was drippy," Totz said, jotting some notes on his notepad.

"Not to worry," Glizzy grumbled. "I know others..."

The trouble was that no other room in Belching Walrus Elementary was any more help.

Baton, Conductor of the Music Room, fell flat. Coach, Head Whistle of the Gym Equipment, could not rally enough spirit.

Chip, Central Processor of the Tech Room, crashed.

"That's everyone I know," Glizzy said as they walked down the hallway. "We'd better get back before we all go stale."

"Hey, Glizzy," Slice said. "I have a question for you."

Glizzy looked at him. His stare sent shivers through Slice's tomato sauce.

"We were just wondering . . . uhh . . ."

Slice was having trouble getting the words out, so Totz jumped in. "We were wondering if a hot dog is a sandwich. You know . . . meat between bread and all . . ."

Glizzy stiffened. "It is a question that goes back generations . . . all the way back to the days of old— the beaches of Corny Island, the ballparks of yore, the pushcarts that dotted every street corner in a place my father called New Pork City."

"We didn't mean to offend you," Slice said.

"Hot dogs certainly are NOT sandwiches,"

Glizzy said. "We are our own thing. Hot dogs are something different."

They walked along in silence. They turned a corner, then another. Behind a closed door, something rumbled.

Slice and Totz looked at each other.

Something rumbled again.

"Quickly," Glizzy said. "We must hide."

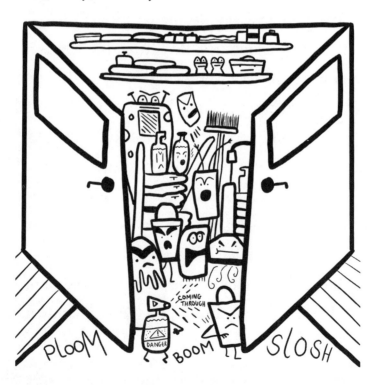

Suddenly, the door burst open, followed by a wave of water that blocked their way. Mops, brooms, buckets, and spray bottles tumbled out and rushed toward them.

"It's the Cleaning Supply Horde," Glizzy said. "They are nothing more than mindless beasts. RUN!!"

But it was too late. The water sloshed forward and soaked Glizzy's bun. He dropped to his knees. Glizzy tried to crawl forward to escape, but . . .

A wet mop slapped down and Glizzy was gone.

CHAPTER 5
Muck Amok about Mustard

Totz jammed his notepad into his pocket and grabbed the mustard packet. He and Slice ran down a hallway and then along another. They twisted and turned every which way. No matter where they went, the screeching horde of cleaning supplies chased them. They ducked a broom, hopped over a mop, and slid under the wheels of a rolling bucket.

"Follow me!" Slice hollered.

They ran down another hallway, but it was a dead end. Long rows of lockers lined the walls. A deep, growly laugh came from a mop as two buckets, six cleaning rags, a push broom, and other cleaning supplies inched toward them.

Slice reached for Totz's hand. "Looks like they're going to wipe us up, buddy."

"Don't give up yet," Totz said. He tossed the mustard packet on the floor.

Slice knew what Totz had in mind.

"THIS IS FOR GLIZZY!" Slice yelled.

They both jumped in the air and stomped on the mustard packet.

The mustard splattered across the floor and against the row of lockers.

The horde's shrieks echoed through the entire school. The cleaning supplies rushed to wipe up the mess. Mops mopped. Brooms swept. Buckets . . . Well, buckets did what buckets do when they're cleaning.

And in the chaos, Slice and Totz slipped through the first door they could find.

"You are not welcome here," a pair of glasses said curtly. She had long brass arms and huge eyes— one in each lens—that never seemed to blink.

"We just ask for safe travel through this place," Slice said, still out of breath from all the excitement.

"What *is* this place?" Totz added.

"I am Spex Bifocals, High Wizard of the Library," the pair of glasses said. "We have heard of your adventures. I must ask you to leave."

"You've heard of us?" Slice couldn't believe anyone had heard of him.

"We at the Library know everything," Spex said. "And we are not able to help you."

"Why not?" Totz asked.

"Look around you. We receive many supplies from the Main Office—paper, pens, clips, staples. If Baron von Lineal found out we helped you, he would cut us off. Anyhow, food is not permitted in the Library. Now please leave immediately."

Slice shuddered. "We can't go back out there. The mops . . . the buckets . . ."

"You know, your shushing is louder than us actually talking," Totz said.

"You will leave immediately," Spex said again. The books stirred even more. "But you have a choice. You may exit the way you came, or you can brave the Labyrinth of Shelves."

"Um . . . What's a labyrinth?" Slice asked.

"RICHARD!" Spex clapped her hand twice and a fat, dusty book wiggled from a shelf. He had a deep blue cover and was almost as thick as he was tall. Huge circles under his eyes hinted at long nights reading in the dim light.

Spex cleared her throat and spoke to the book. "Richard, please define *labyrinth* for these two ignorami."

"What's an ignorami?" Totz whispered.

Suddenly, the book's cover burst open. The pages started turning so quickly, they made a rustling sound.

"Labyrinth is a noun," the book said in a low, rumbly voice. "It is a complicated, irregular network of passages in which it is difficult to find one's way out."

"So, it's a maze," Slice said.

"You could have just said *maze*," Totz added.

Richard grumbled.

"I mean, it's a bunch of walls that go this way and that," Slice said. "You get lost in there."

Richard grumbled louder. His eyes narrowed.

"So, a labyrinth is a maze," Totz said.

"SHHH!!! There is no talking in the Library," Spex said. "I must warn you, though . . . No one who has entered the Labyrinth of Shelves has ever been seen again."

Totz took a step back. "We should go back," he said. "Those shelves look scary."

A knotted, gnarly mop whapped against the Library window, followed by the slaps of four grimy, slimy microfiber rags. Gray nasty liquid oozed down the glass.

"Or the shelves," Totz said. "The shelves sound great."

"We choose the Maze of Shelves," Slice said.

"LABYRINTH!" Spex insisted.

"SHHH!!" Slice and Totz hushed her at once.

The Labyrinth of Shelves seemed endless. As soon as Slice and Totz reached the end of one passageway, it branched and turned in other directions. Soon, they were lost.

"There sure are a lot of books," Totz said. "Just one shelf has a bunch of them. Multiply that by the number of shelves and you have . . ."

"About a gazillion," Slice said.

They turned down another passageway.

"Didn't we come this way before?" Slice asked.

Totz looked around. "I'm not sure. Maybe we should turn back."

As they talked about what to do, they felt a rumble.

"What was that?" Slice said.

A piece of paper floated down and landed on the floor.

The rumbling happened again. A book slid from a high shelf and crashed on the carpet next to them.

Totz touched the book, then looked up.

They both screamed at once.

CHAPTER 6

Ava-Lunch!!

Slice and **Totz ran.** They zigged and zagged in every direction. Books of all colors and sizes thundered down around them.

"Follow me!" Slice said.

They made another turn. More books fell around them.

Totz did a diving roll to avoid a huge hardcover. "Where are you taking us?"

"There!" Slice said. He slid under a book cart.

Bang, bang, bang!!

Books smashed on the metal shelves above them.

"Now push!"

They put their hands on the leg of the book cart and pushed with all their might. The book cart started to roll. They pushed some more and guided the book cart—left, right, then left again—through the Labyrinth of Shelves.

Bang! Boom!! Crunch!!! Smash!!!!

Finally, after what seemed like forever, they saw light at the end of a passage.

"That way!" Totz hollered.

They rolled the cart toward the light. Slice looked up. Richard the dictionary was on the highest shelf. He rocked himself forward until he teetered off.

"Dive!" Slice yelled.

Slice and Totz dove out from under the book cart and rolled out of the Labyrinth of Shelves just

in time. Richard smashed onto the book cart, twist-
ing it into scrap metal. Slice and Totz scrambled
under the nearest library table.

"How do we get out of here?" Slice said. "Spex said food is not allowed in the Library, and I'm fine with that."

"There," Totz said. He climbed up a chair and onto a long desk. He made his way to the far side and pressed a button.

"Scoop," Totz said into a microphone. "Scoop, can you hear me? We're in the Library!"

Totz's voice boomed out of a speaker high on the wall. His voice echoed through every hall and every classroom of Belching Walrus Elementary.

Totz looked over to Slice, who had climbed onto the desk, too. "Is that what my voice sounds like?"

"Do you think Scoop will hear us?" Slice asked.

"She'd better. Or else we're doomed. Everyone knows where we are now."

Books started creeping from the labyrinth. They grunted and moaned as they surrounded the desk and began piling on top of one another.

The speaker on the wall crackled. They could hear Scoop's voice, but her words were broken up.

Totz stomped on the button again. "Help us! Hurry!"

Soon, the books had piled up so high they reached the top of the desk. Spex climbed to the desk-top and started toward them. Richard the dictionary

SLICE... WHERE... TOTZ... DRIP...

and some other books lined up behind her.

"I told you, no one has ever escaped the Labyrinth of Shelves," Spex said.

"We just did," Slice said.

Spex smiled. "No one needs to learn of that, now, do they?"

"We won't tell anyone if you won't," Totz said.

"You just announced it to the whole school," Spex said. "If Baron von Lineal finds out we let you go . . . Well, what would he think?"

More books piled onto the table. Their moaning grew louder.

"He'd think we were clever morsels of food," Slice said.

"He'd think I let you go," Spex said calmly as the books crept closer. "No more paper. No more clips. No more highlighters."

Slice and Totz backed up to the edge of the desk. More books writhed and snarled below. Their covers snapped open and shut like angry freezer bags.

"But that's why we're here," Slice said. "If we can defeat Baron von Lineal together, we can put an end to his evil. He's destroying the Pantry. He's destroying the Cooler. Who's to say the Library won't be next?"

"And if I turn you both to crumbs, what *rewards* will he give us?" Spex said. "SEIZE THEM!"

As the wall of books in front of them got closer and the snarling books below snapped louder, Totz grabbed Slice's trembling hand. "Looks like we're toast, buddy."

Just then, the door to the Library slammed open. Slice and Totz heard a buzzing sound. Two drones whizzed through the air. One was blue and one was green with a pink heart on the side.

"**TARGETS ACQUIRED**," the blue drone said.

"**ACQUIRE TARGETS**," the green drone said.

The drones swooped at the desk. They were fast. Slice worried they might be going too fast. He also worried that Baron von Lineal might have sent them. But what choice did they have?

"Jump!" Slice hollered.

Slice and Totz leaped off the edge of the desk. Slice landed on the blue drone and Totz landed on the green one. The drones whizzed around the Library.

"**I AM BLU1,**" the blue drone said. "**MY COUNTERPART IS GRN1. YOUR SCOOP HAS**

NEGOTIATED AN ALLIANCE WITH THE TECH ROOM."

"OUR DIRECTIVE IS TO BRING YOU BACK TO THE PANTRY," GRN1 said.

"You have not seen the last of Spex Bifocals!"

Spex yelled. "I will look you up! I will mark you down! You'll never be . . ."

But her voice disappeared as the drones rose higher. They could see the Labyrinth of Shelves below.

"It's dangerous," Totz said, "but it's also beautiful."

Slice wiped a tear from his eye. It was the first time he'd had a moment to think in a long while. "Rest in grease, Glizzy," he said. "Rest in grease."

Slice and Totz were silent the rest of the way. They had only known Glizzy for a short time, but somehow, he was a big part of their lives now.

CHAPTER 7
The Blue Meeting

Things back at the Pantry were worse than ever. Cookies had crumbled; juice boxes were squished; eggs had cracked. Smoke rose from the oven. Dented pots and pans lay everywhere.

"This is so non-kosher," Totz said to Slice.

"I'm glad you're back," Scoop said, running over. "I hope you have good news."

Slice looked down. "No matter where we went, the answer was no."

"Everyone at Belching Walrus Elementary is afraid of the Main Office," Totz said.

"Almost everyone," Scoop said. "While you were away, I used the intercom to put out a distress call. I spoke to Chip from the Tech Room. They sent those drones to rescue you."

While they helped clean up, Slice and Totz told Scoop all about their adventures around the

school—the Gym, the Art Room, the Music Room, the horde of cleaning supplies, and the Library. They also talked about Glizzy—about how much of a

help he had been and how they wished they had had more time to get to know him.

Suddenly, sounds came from the door of the Pantry and a long line of food began marching out.

"What's going on?" Totz asked.

"Baron von Lineal called a meeting," Scoop explained. "He asked every room in the school to attend. Sprinkles will be going, along with Chocolate Chip Scone."

"We know more about this than anyone," Slice said. "We should be there."

"I'm coming, too," Scoop said.

"But you'll melt," Totz said.

"Everyone else is risking something," she said. "I can, too."

~~~~~~~~~~~~~~~

Slice, Scoop, and Totz crept into the Auditorium and hid behind a row of seats. Scoop was already feeling a little melty.

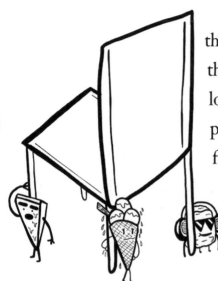

Baron von Lineal sat at the head of a long table on the stage. Behind him, Ducky loomed, along with two staplers. A few representatives from each room sat around the table, too.

Baron von Lineal straightened. "It has come to my attention that some of you have been naughty," he said. "We at the Main Office do not like naughty. We like quiet and obedient. We like orderly and calm."

A few folks shifted uncomfortably in their seats.

Scoop tugged on Slice's arm. She was drippier than ever. "I saw something glint above the stage," she whispered.

THE PANTRY

THE TECH ROOM

THE MUSIC ROOM

THE GYM

BLUE

THE ART ROOM

DIC-
TION-
ARY

THE LIBRARY

Slice ignored her. He was too focused on the meeting.

"Naughty cannot go unpunished," Lineal went on. "Sit here for a few moments to discuss what the right punishment should be."

With that, Baron von Lineal and Ducky marched (or waddled) out of the Auditorium.

The arguments exploded:

Scoop wiped her forehead of melty ice cream. The chocolate and vanilla mixed together to make a sort of wishy-washy tan. She noticed the glint above the stage again and looked closer. Was it metal? A blade? A knife?

Scoop and Totz noticed it, too. They all cried out at once: "Scissors!"

"Snip . . ."

Suddenly, a heavy sandbag fell from the ceiling and crashed down on the table.

Blue Paint splattered.

Coach tweeted loud.

Snare Drum rolled out of the way.

Tennis Ball bounced.

Scoop was leaving puddles of ice cream wherever she went, but she ran to Sprinkles. "Let's get you back to the Pantry."

"My frosting is smudged. My sprinkles have fallen off," Sprinkles wailed. "Leave me here."

"No donut left behind." Slice helped Sprinkles to her feet. He nudged Totz. "Give her a rhyme or two."

Totz whipped out his notepad and flipped a few pages. He had never rhymed in front of anyone but his friends before. "Uh . . . You're frosted, you've been accosted," he said, unsure of himself. "You're awesome, probably exhausted. You feel toasted . . . broiled and roasted. Let's get back to the Pantry before we're composted."

Sprinkles gave a smile and rose to her feet.

"You're right," she said. "We have to get back. We have to show Baron von Lineal that the cream always rises to the top."

By then, the rest of the survivors were stirring and retreating to their rooms.

As they left, Slice heard François call out. "Ze worst zing to happen to Belching Walrus Elementary is ze Cafeteria!!"

No one would ever forget that night in the Auditorium. It would forever be called The Blue Meeting. And it would change all of their lives forever.

CHAPTER 8

Sieging Is Believing

Food from all corners of the Pantry gathered around to hear what happened.

"It was horrible!" Sprinkles sobbed. "I can still hear Kickball bursting as the sandbag landed. Tub of Blue Paint splattered everywhere!"

"We have to prepare," Slice said to Scoop and Totz as they peered out the Pantry door across the Cafeteria.

"Prepare for what?" Totz asked.

"We have to stop Baron von Lineal. It's now or never."

"But what can we do?" Scoop asked. "We're just food. We live peaceful lives."

"And we have to defend our way of life," Slice said. "Otherwise, the Main Office will keep taking more and more. Think of the pickles."

Just then, they heard the sound of marching in the distance. Baron von Lineal rode through the Cafeteria door atop Ducky. His army of pens, staplers, and pencils followed. Two large tape dispensers brought up the rear.

They all chanted in unison: "RULER RULE . . . RULER RULE . . . RULER RULE . . ."

The army filed into the Cafeteria and lined up in orderly rows. Then they went silent.

"If the Pantry will not give us use of the Cooler willingly, we will take it by force," Lineal said.

"WE WILL TAKE IT BY FORCE!" a stapler repeated.

"Hoo-hah!" the entire army roared at once.

Panic spread through the Pantry. Bananas peeled out. Potatoes felt fried. Ice melted.

But Slice was right. They had to do something. He tugged on a lunch tray. "Let's go. I have a plan."

Scoop and Totz had no idea what Slice was up to, but they knew doing something was better than doing nothing. They grabbed hold of the tray and pulled. It began to move. They dragged the tray to the edge of the counter. Finally, Slice gave it one last shove.

The tray fell and clattered in front of the door to the Pantry. He was building a barrier!

"It won't stop them, but it might slow them down." Slice panted. "Let's get more."

They dragged another tray across the counter and let it fall. They dropped tray after tray. Before long, there was a pile of trays in front of the Pantry door.

"We're not done yet," Scoop said, hopping onto a large bin. She picked up pats of butter, peeled off the foil wrapping, and tossed them to the tile below.

While Scoop did that, Totz jammed a plastic spoon between the edge of the counter and a cart. He bent it back and placed a pepper packet in it. "It's a catapult," he said.

"More like a *pepper-pult*," Slice said.

Just then, Totz's grip slipped and he let go of the spoon.

The packet of black pepper silently lobbed from the counter and landed at the feet of a fat yellow highlighter. The packet broke open and a cloud of pepper poofed into the air . . .

"Ah . . ."

"Ahhh . . ."

"Achooo!"

The highlighter gave a sneeze.

"Such aggression cannot go unpunished," Baron von Lineal announced. "Charge!"

"HOO-HAH!" The entire army of the Main Office charged toward the Pantry.

Staplers slipped as Scoop tossed more pats of butter off the edge. Pens and pencils sneezed as Totz and Slice lobbed more pepper.

Suddenly, two eggs showed up. "Sal and Monella reporting for duty!" they said at once.

Slice looked down at the little eggs. "You guys are too fragile," he said. "Why don't you go back to your crate and stay safe?"

"We are here because we *are* fragile, sir," Sal said.

"We'll be scrambled if Baron von Lineal wins," Monella added.

Slice and Totz looked at each other. "Okay," Slice said. "You two work the pepper-pult. Scoop, Totz, and I have a job to do."

Just then, something slapped Scoop on the side of the head and fell to the counter. It was a rubber band. Another one slapped Totz, and then Slice. The pencils were firing rubber bands from the back row.

"That kinda stings," Totz said.

"Yeah, very unpleasant," Scoop agreed.

By now, staplers were working to move the lunch trays while tape was slowly creeping up the front of the counter toward them. Pens and pencils climbed behind them. Meanwhile, Baron von Lineal sat atop Ducky enjoying the view.

"You have no chance," Baron von Lineal called out.

"YOU HAVE NO CHANCE!" a stapler repeated.
"Surrender now and I will be merciful!"
"SURRENDER NOW AND—"

"Stop repeating everything I say!" Baron von Lineal whined.

As Sal and Monella flung pepper, Slice, Scoop, and Totz searched for something, anything, to slow down the Main Office. It would only be moments before they moved the lunch trays and opened the Pantry door.

CHAPTER 9
Oil's Well that Eggs Well

Here!" **Scoop called** out. She had found a plastic jug of cooking oil at the edge of the counter. "The tape won't be able to get up here if the front of the counter is slippery."

They pushed and shoved at the jug. They leaned into it and kicked it.

"It's no use," grunted Slice. "It won't budge!"

"SNIP!"

They all turned around.

Snip the scissors was standing there. She had silently climbed the side of the counter.

"Ssso," she said. "It appearsss your resssissstance isss at an end. Sssurender now and we will be merciful."

"Never," Slice said. "You've ruined the whole Cafeteria."

"You've put us all in danger," Scoop added.

"It'sss you who hurtsss the ssschool," Snip said, inching closer. "Food in the Library damagesss booksss. Drinksss in the Tech Room friesss computersss. Ice Cream dripsss everywhere, upsssetting the Cleaning Sssupply Horde. It'sss time to ssstop you!"

And with that, Snip leaped forward.

"SNIP!!!"

The cooking oil gushed out of the jug and glugged across the counter. Slice, Totz, and Scoop ran to the edge. Scoop grabbed a dish towel and they leaped.

Oil spilled from the jug. The more Snip strug-
gled to get out, the faster it came. Soon, oil poured
off the edge of the counter. It dripped, oozed, and
drizzled its way down the sheer wall. Pepper continued to fly across the Cafeteria, and they could hear
Sal and Monella working hard.

"Heave!"

"Ho!"

"Heave!"

"Ho!"

With each *ho* another pepper lobbed across the Cafeteria. With each pepper lob, more pens sneezed.

"The eggs haven't left their posts," Scoop said.

"The oil will get them," Totz added.

"Sal! Monella!" Slice hollered. "Jump!"

Their domed little heads peeked over the edge of the counter.

"Jump!" Totz said.

"It's too far. We'll crack!" Monella said.

Scoop grabbed the dish towel, handed one end to Totz, and stretched it out. "We'll catch you!" she said.

Suddenly, Snip loomed behind them. "I'll poach you!"

Sal and Monella jumped. Monella was on target and landed in the center of the towel.

Maybe his glasses fogged up. Maybe it was against every instinct for an egg to leap off a high counter. Maybe he was just a bad jumper. In any event, Sal missed the towel and headed straight for the tile.

"I've got him!" Slice dove across the floor and caught Sal just before he cracked.

Meanwhile, the oil continued to drip. And tape dispensers started to slip.

"Watch out!" Totz called out as tape dispensers smashed to the floor around them.

They all dove to the side, scampering past the last of the lunch trays and bursting through the Pantry door. Baron von Lineal's army began to flood in as well.

"There are too many of them!" Totz said.

"We need to retreat," Slice said.

"Where will we go?" Scoop asked.

Slice looked around and had an idea. He hopped onto a milk crate. "TO THE COOLER!" he hollered. "Food can last a long time in the Cooler!"

Bananas and oranges, ice creams and yogurts, and chocolate milks and muffins all ran into the Cooler. Apple pulled the door closed with a *SLAM*!

The murmuring was so loud it pushed the

boundaries of how loud a murmur can get before becoming noise.

"We're trapped," one french fry said to the others in the box. The rest of them cried.

"We can stay in here as long as we like," Slice said. "We're food. We stay fresh in the Cooler."

"SNIP."

Just then, the power went out. The only light

came through the small window at the top of the door. Slice, Scoop, and Totz peered out.

Baron von Lineal, Ducky, and Snip were standing

near the outlet. Snip had snipped the electrical cord.

"We have a problem," Totz said.

CHAPTER 10

Food Fight!

This time, the murmur was not a murmur. It was a total freak-out.

"This is definitely not good," Scoop said. "Milk will spoil. I'll melt. The little chicken nugs will thaw."

"No chance," Slice reassured her. "It's time to make a stand."

"But there are a million of them out there," Totz said, peering out the window.

"And the pepper-pult only slowed them down," Monella said.

Slice looked down at the panicking food. They were running in every direction.

"Hang on," he said.

Slice climbed down from the window and jumped into a nearby carton. The box jostled around a bit, and he came back out.

"Everyone, settle down!" Slice hollered.

But no one listened, they just ran around in a total freak-out.

"Scoop," Slice said, "make a painting, a huge mural on the window."

"What will that do?"

"There's no time to explain," Slice said. "Monella, Sal, do you have any pepper left?"

"We've got a few packets," Sal said.

"Great, when I give you the signal, toss it in the air like confetti."

Slice turned to Totz. "Are you ready to rock a rhyme like never before?"

Totz looked down at the crowd. "No."

"Come on," Slice said. "This is your big chance."

"I already told you . . . I don't want a big chance."

"Who doesn't want a big chance?" Slice urged. "Pull out that pad and weave your words."

Totz pulled out his notepad and scribbled a few things down. He scratched some things out, and thought some more.

Meanwhile, Scoop was blotting and splatting her ice cream on the window. As it dripped down, the light from outside shone through, sending swirling colors across the Cooler.

The beautiful colors seemed to settle the food down. Heads began to turn toward the window.

Totz took a deep breath, looked at his friends, and said, "Okay, let's give this a go."

"Ladies and gentlemen!" Slice called out. More food settled down, more heads turned. "May I present to you the Warlock of Words, the Prince of Poetry, the Ruler of Rhymes, the . . . uhh . . . the Sultan of . . . uh . . . Stanzas, the one and only TOTZ!!!"

Totz looked at Slice and Scoop.

Slice urged him to start.

Totz started to pace around the stage.

Suddenly, a huge *BANG* sounded. Then another *BANG*! Then another.

Slice looked out the window. Baron von Lineal was just outside the Cooler atop Ducky. They were ramming against the door trying to break it down.

Bang, boom . . . Bang–bang, boom . . .

Bang, boom . . . Bang–bang, boom . . .

Bang, boom . . . Bang–bang, boom . . .

The rhythm of the banging got Totz going. He began to march in time to the beat, his head bobbing. Then he weaved his rhymes.

"We used to sit 'round and hang in the Cooler.
But along came the Main Office with Baron von Ruler.
We welcomed them in to share in some giggles.
'Til the paperweight went and knocked off the pickles."

Upon hearing their names, the pickles all perked up and began cheering.

Other food started getting excited, clapping their hands and stomping their feet. Totz glanced at his notepad and went on.

"Me and Slice, we went out for assistance.
Scoop stayed here and helped the resistance.
We traveled the school until we were dizzy.
Then the mop slapped down and took out old Glizzy."

Slice pointed to Sal and Monella who tossed extra pepper in the air.

Cheers rose up from the crowd. And there was no sneezing. (You probably already knew food is immune to the effects of pepper.)

The door started to buckle from Ducky's pounding, but Totz didn't notice. He was stomping in time with the beat now. His voice rose higher.

"Art Room, Music, Gym, they ain't helping.
Library threw some books from the shelving.
Cleaning Supplies tried to wipe us out.
But my crew is tougher than brussels sprouts."

At the mention of brussels sprouts, the entire fresh food section went wild.

Scoop splattered some strawberry ice cream across the window, sending rays of pink through the Cooler. The cheering rose even louder. The door bent and buckled even more, but there was no stopping Totz now.

"We're facing those thugs who grab what they want.
Donut, chips, scones, or chocolate croissants.
Things look grim, there's no way to fake it.
But the whole pie's ours if we just go and bake it!"

By then, the whole Cooler was rocking to the beat, cheering and stomping. And the riled-up food burst from the Cooler. They were going to stop Baron von Lineal and his army of office supplies once and for all!

CHAPTER 11
The Final Fray

The battle was legendary. Ice cubes slid across the tile into pink erasers. Rubber bands flew through the air. Oranges were dumped from high shelves. Pencils poked at tender meat loaf.

"We are completely outnumbered!" Sprinkles called out, a highlighter cap sailing right through her donut hole.

"Keep fighting!" Slice said, sliding across the floor and slapping into a staple remover.

Totz rallied the rest of the tater tots. He led them in taking down a tape dispenser.

Scoop spun around, sending melted ice cream in every direction. It splatted in the faces of a whole row of red pens.

But no matter how hard they fought, the office supplies were stronger. Baron von Lineal laughed as he ordered his forces around. Slowly, food was being pushed back, back, back.

"It's hopeless," Scoop said. "We're just softer than office supplies."

Slice deflected a paper clip with his pepperoni armor. He pulled off a few pieces and flung them. They slapped over Ducky's eyes.

Ducky reared up, sending Baron von Lineal to the floor.

"No matter," Lineal said. "I don't need Ducky to win. He's always been dead weight, anyway. The Cooler is ours!"

Ducky lumbered away.

Slice knew they had to fight Baron von Lineal, but it was starting to feel hopeless.

Suddenly, a whistle tweeted and a holler echoed across the Cafeteria. "This is for all the Leftovers!"

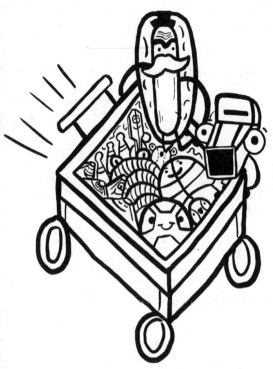

It was Glizzy. He was alive! He was riding atop a wagon filled with the Gym Equipment. Coach was by his side.

"It's true," Totz said in awe. "Hot dogs are not mere sandwiches. They're something different."

"They *are* their own thing," Slice said.

Glizzy gave a war cry. "I will *relish* defeating you, Baron von Lineal!"

Balls bounced through Lineal's army, scattering pens and pencils in every direction. One orange cone tottered in and fell on a row of staplers.

"How did you get the Gym Equipment to join us?" Slice called out.

"A healthy body starts with a balanced meal, son," Glizzy said.

Coach tweeted again. "We couldn't stand by and watch good food go to waste."

That gave Slice an idea. "Scoop! Totz! Meet me at the intercom."

Slice hopped on a milk crate, climbed a dish-rag, and pulled himself up next to the cash register.

The intercom looked complicated. He didn't know what to do.

"This one," Scoop said, stomping on a red button. "Talk into that."

By then, Totz had climbed to the counter, too. He jumped on top of the giant microphone.

"Are you ready to go worldwide?" Slice asked Totz.

"What choice do I have?" He took a deep breath and belted out lyrics.

"To all the rooms at Belching Walrus.
I've got news that'll make you nauseous.
We've been attacked by the Main Office.
We need your help, but please be cautious!"

Scoop stepped up next to him and gave it a try:

"Markers, brushes, and tubs of paste.
I've got news that'll make you faint.
The Main Office already squashed Blue Paint.
So come down here, show no restraint!"

Totz stepped up to the microphone for another verse, this one for the Music Room:

"From the piccolos to the biggest drum.
I've got news that'll make you hum.
The Baron wants us under his thumb.
So change your tune before we're crumbs!"

"We need a final verse," Totz said. "We have to reach the Library."

"Spex, High Wizard of Library, and Richard the dictionary?" Slice said. "They won't come. They're maniacs."

"We need all the help we can get," Scoop said.

"Don't look at me," Slice said. "I'm terrible at rhyming."

Totz sighed, flipped a few pages, and belted out another verse:

"I'm reaching out to every book.
I have news that ain't gobbledygook.
Baron von Lineal is a crook.
So turn a page before we're cooked!"

Within moments, they heard a buzzing sound. Drones from the Tech Room flew in. They carried paintbrushes and magic markers from the Art Room. They carried flutes and drumsticks from the Music Room. They even carried books from the Library!

Then a tuba and a robot marched through the door. Tubs of red, yellow, and green paint waddled across the floor. Richard the dictionary lumbered in with Spex Bifocals at his side. The Cafeteria was flooded with items from all over the school.

"We couldn't let you have all ze fun!" François the paintbrush said.

"That would be an error," Chip said.

The battle raged on and the mess became worse. Ink spilled; ketchup and mustard splattered. But even with the help, things began to look bleak.

"What are we going to do?" Scoop said.

Totz looked from Scoop to Slice, then back to Scoop, then back to Slice. Then he looked back to Scoop and then back to Slice.

"Are you going to say something?" Slice asked.

"I have an idea, but it might be dangerous," Totz explained.

As he whispered his idea to his friends, Sal, Monella, and Glizzy showed up.

"What are you standing around for?" Glizzy said. "We need every man, woman, and potato skin down there!"

"Yeah, we're getting fried," Monella said.

"We need to get everyone back into the Cooler," Slice told them. "It's time to run away."

"Run away?" Glizzy growled. "You can't be serious."

"The only way to win is to run away," Scoop said.

"You're not making sense, son," Glizzy said, "but I'm going to trust you on this."

"Look down there," Totz said. "We're doomed anyhow."

Glizzy spread his hot dog bun and leaped off the counter. He landed on a robot, which began beeping and flashing.

"To the Cooler!" he bellowed. "Retreat!"

Baton lifted and began conducting his instruments.

Coach tweeted and gave orders to the Gym Equipment.

Robots, drones, and every microchip acted in unison.

Spex ordered her forces to file away.

They all began fleeing to the Cooler.

Totz stood tall on the microphone and nodded to Scoop. "Press the button."

Just then, a paper clip hit Totz in the back of his starchy head.

"You've been clipped!" the paper clip cried out in a squeaky voice.

Totz fell from the microphone and tumbled to the floor below.

POK!

"Totz!" Slice called out. But he was gone, swallowed up by the gaping mouth of a passing tuba. The tuba lumbered into the Cooler and disappeared.

Scoop turned to Slice. "It's up to you," she said.

"I can't rhyme," Slice said.

"We have no choice," Scoop said. "Now get up there!"

Sal tossed a handful of pepper in the air. "Yeah, go for it."

Slice stood next to the microphone. He cleared his throat and spoke:

"There's a major mess in the Cafeteria.
We need help . . . uh . . . to stop bacteria.
It's the dirtiest place in . . . the whole . . . area.
Better hurry before . . . um . . . we get diphtheria?"

It wasn't the best verse in the history of verses, but it was the only thing Slice could think of.

And it was enough.

A piercing screech filled the halls of Belching Walrus Elementary. Within moments, mops, brooms, buckets, and rags flooded into the Cafeteria. Mops mopped. Brooms swept. Rags wiped. And buckets bucketed.

"Hurry," Slice said.

They scurried down from the counter and across the floor toward the Cooler.

"Hurry!" Glizzy called out.

"Hurry!" Scoop said.

"Hurry!" Totz screamed from the Cooler. "We have to shut the door!"

Slice, Scoop, and the rest of them dodged mops, slid past brooms, and flipped over buckets. They made their way to the Cooler and ran inside.

"You cannot stop us!" Baron von Lineal bellowed. "We'll be back. We rule the whole school. Belching Walrus is OURS!"

Red the apple heaved on the heavy door. "It's stuck," Red said.

A mop saw the mess in the Cooler and came toward them, growling.

"Pull harder!" Scoop said.

"It won't budge!" Red grunted.

Just then, a flash of brass glinted. It was Ducky!

He threw his weight against the Cooler door. Red pulled again, and the door slammed shut.

THOOM!

They scampered to the window and looked out.

The office supplies were being mopped and swept and wiped up as though a tidal wave was crashing through the Cafeteria. Within moments, the cleaning supplies disappeared and the Cafeteria was sparkling clean.

Cheers rose throughout the cramped Cooler. Books high-fived muffins. Magic markers shook hands

with clarinets. Robots beeped, bopped, and booped.

Glizzy and Sprinkles rushed over.

"Great job!" Glizzy said.

"Yes," Sprinkles added. "You are all great heroes."

"I don't feel like a hero." Slice sighed. "I just feel like sitting down and catching my breath."

CHAPTER 12

Dessert Time

No one had seen a single office supply for days. And each night, every other resident at Belching Walrus Elementary came to the Cafeteria to hang out.

Glizzy and Sprinkles called for a meeting. They asked all to attend. Before long, the Cooler was filled with everyone from every room—the Cafeteria, the Gym, the Art Room, the Music Room, the Tech Room, and the Library alike.

"We all fought hard," Glizzy said. "We all helped out. But a few of you rose above and beyond the call of *fruity*."

"We want to thank you," Sprinkles added.

"First off," Glizzy said. "BLU1 and GRN1, drones of the finest components. Thank you for rescuing Slice and Totz from certain doom."

"Next," Sprinkles said, "we want to thank Coach, Head Whistle of the Gym Equipment, the first group to help out. You risked so much. It couldn't have been easy."

"Sal and Monella," Glizzy said. "Two of the toughest eggs I've ever met. You didn't crack under pressure."

"Totz and Scoop," Sprinkles said. "Your words and your art not only lifted us up when we felt hopeless, but they helped rally support when we needed it most."

"And last but not least," Glizzy said. "Slice . . . You knew what had to be done when no one else could see it. You inspired us all when we saw no way out. You have the heart and mind of a true leader."

Slice's cheeks turned redder than the pepperoni on his cheesy chest.

Cheers rose from the audience. Horns tooted. Whistles tweeted. Robots beeped, bopped, and booped. Books rifled their pages.

When things settled down, everyone looked to Slice to say a few words.

"Thank you, thank you," he said. "I wasn't looking for any special attention. I just knew someone needed to do something. We learned a lot and made new friends along the way. And that knowledge and those new friendships helped us solve our problems."

"So I want to thank each and every one of you for your bravery, your dedication, and your commitment to making Belching Walrus Elementary safe and fair for everyone."

Another cheer rose up, this one louder than the first.

A knock sounded on the Cooler door. Everyone looked around, worried.

Scoop peered out the window. "Open the door," she said.

"But the last time someone knocked, it was Baron von Lineal," Sprinkles said. "It's what got us into that whole mess in the first place."

Totz looked out the window and nodded. "Yeah, open it."

Red heaved on the Cooler door. Ducky waddled in alone.

A murmur spread throughout the Cooler. A tuba let out a low toot.

"Ducky saved us," Slice said. "He helped us when we needed it most."

"Ducky," Glizzy said in his grizzled old voice, "anyone who stands against their friends when they see injustice is the greatest hero of all. You are welcome here any time."

A cheer rose up among everyone at Belching Walrus Elementary.

In the whole history of brass paperweights shaped like a duck, Ducky smiled bigger than any brass paperweight shaped like a duck ever had before.

"And before this goes on too long," Slice said, "I think we should bust out with a song."

Slice looked at Totz, Scoop, Sal, and Monella.

They all smiled.